Hebron Public Library
201 W. Sigler Street
Hebron, IN 46341

Richard III

Published by Sweet Cherry Publishing Limited
Unit 36, Vulcan House,
Vulcan Road,
Leicester, LE5 3EF
United Kingdom

First published in the US in 2013
2020 hardback edition

2 4 6 8 10 9 7 5 3

ISBN: 978-1-78226-728-7

© Sweet Cherry Publishing

Richard III

Based on the original story from William Shakespeare,
adapted by Kellie Jones.

Lexile® code numerical measure L = Lexile® 1130L

Guided Reading Level = T

Cover design and illustrations by Vishnu Madhav

www.sweetcherrypublishing.com

Printed and bound in India
I.TP002

About Shakespeare

William Shakespeare, regarded as the greatest writer in the English language, was born in Stratford-upon-Avon in Warwickshire, England, in 1564. He was the third of eight children born to John and Mary Shakespeare.

Shakespeare was a poet, playwright and dramatist. He is often known as England's national poet and the "Bard of Avon." Thirty-eight plays, one hundred and fifty-four sonnets, two long narrative poems and several other poems are attributed to him. Shakespeare's plays have been translated into every major existent language and are performed more often than those of any other playwright.

Richard: He is the younger brother of King Edward IV and the Duke of Clarence. In the peace after the House of York has beaten Lancaster, he is jealous of his brothers and bitter about his deformed back and arm. At the start of the play he is Duke of Gloucester but through murder and manipulation he becomes King Richard III.

Queen Elizabeth: She is the wife
of King Edward IV and mother of
the "Princes in the Tower" and the
princess whom Richard later plans
to marry. She has two sons from
a previous marriage and Richard
tauntingly uses her former name of
"Lady Grey." Richard uses mistrust
of her family to his advantage.

Duke of Buckingham: He is Richard's ally until he refuses to murder Richard's nephews, the young princes. In return for his help,

Richard promises to make him Earl of Hereford but the former queen, Margaret, warns Buckingham to expect betrayal.

Queen Margaret: She is the widow of King Henry VI, who died at the end of the civil war. She curses Elizabeth for taking her crown and Richard for

killing her husband and son. It is her widowed daughter-in-law, Lady Anne, whom Richard marries first.

Richard III

In the peace following years of civil war between the royal families of York and Lancaster, there lived a hunchbacked man with a withered hand and a jealous heart. His name was Richard, Duke of Gloucester.

His side, the Yorkists,
had finally won the
battle to rule England.

"Now is the winter
of our discontent made
glorious summer by this
son of York," he said.

Triumph was theirs
and all around people
celebrated—yet Richard was
not happy. He wanted to be
king himself, but instead his
older brother Edward now
sat upon the throne. Unable
to enjoy the pleasures of
peace or find a woman who
could accept his deformity,
Richard determined to
take the crown for himself.

He vowed to manipulate and murder whoever he must to get it: starting by setting his other brother, the Duke of Clarence, and the king against each other.

Richard circulated a prophecy that someone whose name began with "G" would murder King Edward's heirs.

Soon after, the Duke of Clarence
was arrested and imprisoned in
the Tower of London. When
Richard pretended not to know
why, Clarence reminded him that
his first name was "George" and
the king feared that *he* would be
the one to murder his children.
Richard blamed this on the king's

wife, Queen Elizabeth: "'Tis not the king that sends you to the Tower. My Lady Grey his wife, Clarence, 'tis she."

Richard also accused the queen of working with her brother to imprison Lord Hastings, who was being set free that day. The queen, he insisted, was manipulating the king. Because of her, no one was safe. Promising to help Clarence, Richard waited until he was alone to declare that he loved his brother so much he would soon send him to heaven in death.

Just then, the newly released
Lord Hastings delivered the
news that the king was gravely
ill. Richard promised to follow
Lord Hastings in visiting the king
later. He resolved that he would
secretly encourage him to execute
Clarence so that when the king
also died, Richard would be closer

to the throne. He then planned
to marry Lady Anne Neville from
the House of Lancaster, even
though he had recently killed her
husband and her father-in-law, the
former King Henry VI.

King Henry VI's
coffin was carried
through the streets

where his grieving widow Queen
Margaret and daughter-in-law,
Lady Anne, cursed the killer
and wished that his children be
deformed and his wife miserable.
Richard interrupted the funeral
procession to declare his love for
Anne, a love so strong it drove
him to kill her husband. At first

Lady Anne was disgusted, but she softened when he begged her to kill him or let him kill himself if she would not marry him. Finally, believing that he was sorry for his evil deeds, she agreed.

At the royal palace, Queen Elizabeth was worried what would happen if the king died. She

did not want Richard to become
the guardian of her young son,
who would inherit the throne.
Two noblemen, the Duke of
Buckingham and Lord Stanley,
reported that the king seemed to
be feeling better and wanted to
meet with Richard and the queen's
brothers to make peace between
them. Elizabeth accused Richard
of hating her and her family ever

since she switched sides after the Lancastrians lost the war, and Richard accused Elizabeth of orchestrating the imprisonment of both Clarence and Lord Hastings.

The former queen, Margaret, entered unnoticed as they argued. She blamed Elizabeth for the theft of her crown and Richard for the death of her husband and son. Meanwhile Earl Rivers, Queen Elizabeth's brother, who benefited greatly from her marriage, insisted that they were not traitors but loyal followers of whoever was king.

"Hear me, you wrangling pirates," said the old queen, Margaret, who thought they were all as bad as each other. To Richard she claimed, "A husband and a son thou ow'st to me"; to Queen Elizabeth, "And thou a kingdom." She cursed Elizabeth to live to see her own children die and another woman take her throne. She hoped Elizabeth's brother, Lord Rivers, and her son from a previous marriage, Lord Grey, would die too. Queen Margaret cursed them and Lord Hastings for standing by as her son was murdered. Richard she condemned to be plagued with suspicions and to believe his friends were traitors while taking traitors as his closest friends.

Lastly she warned Buckingham
that Richard would betray him.

A nobleman called Catesby
who served Richard brought
the news that the king wished
to see them all. Richard was
pleased that he had managed
to convince so many that

Queen Elizabeth was to blame for Clarence's imprisonment. He sent two murderers to kill Clarence immediately. Meanwhile the sickly King Edward IV greeted his visitors and urged them to be friends. They all agreed, but when Queen Elizabeth asked the king to accept

Clarence back into his good
graces, Richard revealed that
he was already dead. Everyone
was shocked, especially King
Edward, who had sent a message
to pardon Clarence. His health
became worse and he soon died.

Buckingham agreed with
Richard that they should protect
the young prince and future king
from the bad influence of his

mother and her followers. Soon
after, the queen learned that
Earl Rivers, Lord Grey, and her

friend Sir Thomas Vaughan had
been imprisoned. She thought
she and her children would be
targeted next. The Cardinal
granted sanctuary to Queen
Elizabeth but Buckingham
insisted that her other royal son,
the young prince's brother, should
attend the coronation. Until

then, Richard suggested that both children stay in the Tower for their safety.

Since the prince was too young to rule, Richard had become Lord Protector of England, but he wanted more. Richard, Buckingham and Catesby plotted to make Richard king instead. However, Catesby was concerned that Lord Hastings would not support them, even though he and Richard were friends. Hastings hated the queen's family, but had loved the late King Edward IV. Furthermore,

Lord Stanley would do whatever
Hastings did. If Hastings
did not cooperate, Richard
declared, "Chop off his head!"

Richard planned to
execute the queen's captive
followers the next day and even

though he was not yet king, he
promised to give Buckingham
the earldom of Hereford for all
his help. Catesby had been sent
to convince Lord Hastings to
support Richard's claim to the
throne. Hastings was happy to
learn that the queen's family

were to be killed but could not support his friend Richard taking the crown from the young prince.

Earl Rivers, Lord Grey, and Sir Thomas Vaughan were executed. Before he died, Rivers prayed that Richard, Hastings and Buckingham would soon meet their share of

35

Queen Margaret's curse, but that Queen Elizabeth and her children would be spared.

At a council meeting to discuss the coronation of the young king, the assembly decided to crown him the next day. Richard and Buckingham talked privately of Hastings refusing to join their scheme, while Hastings continued to believe that Richard was good and true.

When Richard returned from his talk he was furious, claiming to have learned that his deformed arm was a result of witchcraft cast against him by Queen Elizabeth. He accused Hastings of conspiring

with her and ordered his execution: "Off with his head!"

Hastings's head was brought before the Lord Mayor. Richard and Buckingham pretended to be sad over the treachery, and the mayor was convinced that Hastings must have deserved execution

without trial, even though he
did not hear his confession.

Richard ordered Buckingham
to spread the rumor that King
Edward's sons were illegitimate
and not rightful heirs to the

throne. The citizens were not
convinced and didn't seem to
want Richard to become king.
To mend his bad reputation,
Richard pretended that he
would not take the crown if
the public did not want him
to. Buckingham made a speech
saying it would be treason for
Richard not to save England
from the rule of an illegitimate

heir. Still Richard
pretended to feel
reluctant and unworthy.
Finally Buckingham
declared that this was
because Richard loved
his nephew too much
to depose him, but that
he must—for the good
of the people. Finally,
Richard agreed and
was hailed Richard III,
King of England.

Queen Elizabeth
and her companions were
prevented from visiting
the princes in the Tower
and learned that Richard
was now king and soon

to be married to Lady Anne
Neville. Like Elizabeth, Anne
believed that she was the victim
of a curse: her own. In wishing
that Richard's wife would be
unhappy, she had damned
herself as she had no choice
but to marry him. She worried
that Richard would soon kill
her. Lord Stanley, who brought
the news, was worried that his
stepson, the Earl of Richmond,

could be in danger since he was also in line for the throne. He promised to send word to warn him and to ask him to give protection to anyone escaping England and its new king.

True to the old queen Margaret's curse, Richard

was a paranoid king. When
Buckingham could not bring
himself to murder the two
princes, Richard replaced him
with Sir James Tyrell. Richard
had learned that the Marquess
of Dorset, the former queen
Elizabeth's other son, had fled

to join Richmond. With the princes dead, Richard planned to marry their sister to strengthen his kingship, but first he ordered Catesby to spread a rumor that Queen Anne was deathly ill.

Richard ignored Buckingham's reminder that

he was supposed to be given
the earldom of Hereford for his
loyal service and Buckingham
decided to flee to Wales before
he ended up like Hastings.
Already predicting a civil war
with Richmond, especially
since King Henry VI had

once predicted that Richmond
would become king, Richard
warned Lord Stanley not to let
his wife, Richmond's mother,
send any letters to her son.

Tyrell returned and reported
that the princes were dead.
He had hired two other men
to do it since even he could

not bring himself to smother
children. Richard was delighted
and promised to reward Tyrell
handsomely. Meanwhile Queen
Anne had died and Richard
had imprisoned Clarence's son
and married off his daughter so
that neither would be threats
to his crown. Richmond was

gaining support so Richard set out to start wooing his niece knowing that Richmond wanted to marry her himself. He even asked Queen Elizabeth to speak to her daughter on his behalf.

More and more people abandoned Richard's side to join Richmond's. When Lord Stanley brought a report that

Richmond had arrived to seize
the throne, Richard accused him
of helping the enemy—why else
had he not brought troops with
him? Richard sent him to gather
his men but demanded that he
leave his son behind as insurance

that those men would fight *for*
Richard and not against him.

Lord Stanley held a secret
meeting with a priest on
Richmond's side. He could not
fight with them openly without
endangering his son, but he sent
word from Queen Elizabeth

that she would be happy for
Richmond to marry her daughter.

Richmond's army made
camp near Richard's at Bosworth
Field in Leicester. Richard was
pleased that Richmond had
far fewer troops than he did,
but Richmond's men had been
strengthened by speeches of hope

and peace, while Richard's men were unhappy and fearful. Among Richard's men was Lord Stanley, who had been passing information to his stepson. Richard had instructed Lord Stanley to bring his troops before sunrise, "lest his son George fall into the blind cave of eternal night." So

Lord Stanley went secretly to
Richmond's camp and told him
to be prepared for battle early next
morning. He promised to mislead
Richard's troops in
whatever way he could,
while still appearing to
be loyal for the safety
of his captive son.

That night
Richard, who drank
wine and slept early,
was visited by the
ghosts of all those
he had killed, who
condemned him to
"Despair and die!" To
Richmond, who had
made his preparations

long into the night, the same ghosts bade him to "Awake, and win the day." Richard knew that he was a villain and refused to

pity himself, but the dream had
frightened him as it foretold
that this would be his final
battle. Meanwhile Richmond's
dream had encouraged him
and he led his troops into
battle with a rousing speech.

Richard's speech was far
less inspiring and interrupted

by news that Lord Stanley
would not be bringing his
troops after all. There was
no time for Richard to kill
Stanley's son before the battle,
so he vowed to do it after—
but he never got the chance.

On the battlefield Richard
hunted for Richmond on foot

crying "A horse, a horse, my kingdom for a horse!" Finally, after killing several decoys, Richard found the real Richmond. The two fought fiercely and Richard was slain. Lord Stanley plucked the crown from his body and Richmond was crowned King Henry VII. All the soldiers who had fought so unwillingly on the tyrant Richard's side were forgiven and England was unified. With the marriage of the new king from the

Lancastrian line to the daughter
of Queen Elizabeth and the late
King Edward IV of the line of
York the War of the Roses was
finally over after thirty-two years.